Y0-BBW-922

THE MOVIE STORYBOOK

Adapted by Benjamin Harper

Superman created by Jerry Siegel and Joe Shuster

Copyright © DC Comics 2006. First edition.
Printed in the United States of America. All rights reserved.
ISBN: 0-696-22901-3

Superman and all related names, characters and
elements are trademarks of DC Comics.
© 2006. All Rights Reserved.
Visit DC Comics at www.dckids.com

We welcome your comments and suggestions. Write to us at: Meredith Books, Children's Books,
1716 Locust St., Des Moines, IA 50309-3023

meredithbooks.com

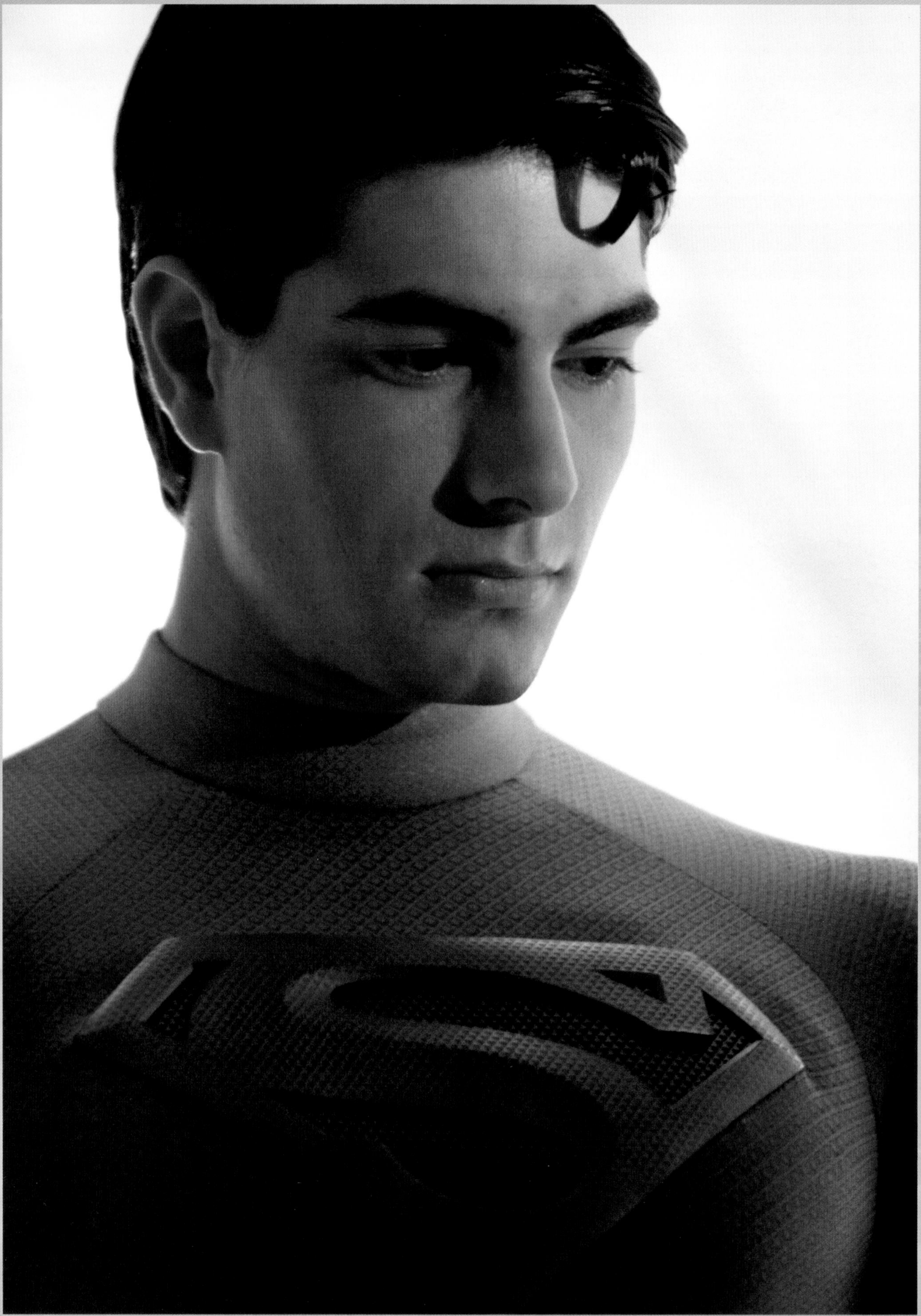

The crystal ship zoomed through space, its sole occupant dormant in a sleep pod. Soaring past stars toward its destination, the ship awakened its sleeping passenger with an alarm. A star chart appeared, showing Superman that he was nearing the end of his journey—what he hoped would be the planet Krypton. Could astronomers' reports that his home planet was still intact and showing signs of life be true?

Touching a crystal on the control panel, Superman turned off the alarm. With the touch of another crystal, he opened a transparent panel so he could see what was outside. All Superman could see was a darkness so vast that it blocked out the stars.

Turning on a massive beam from his spacecraft, Superman illuminated what was in front of him—a huge, black planet. His hopes rising that Krypton actually had survived the blast that allegedly destroyed it so many decades before, Superman brought his spacecraft in for a closer look.

Crystal cities, monuments, and canyons came into view, but there was something wrong. They looked dark and quiet, not bright and glowing, as cities should be.

Something else was wrong too. Superman was beginning to tremble and he felt slightly sick. A single bead of sweat dripped from his brow as he tried to fight off the sensations and move on.

Superman maneuvered his craft through the broken ruins of a massive dome and descended into a deep canyon. Large monoliths were arranged in a circle around the perimeter of the canyon. As Superman inspected the monoliths, he noticed that a hieroglyph was carved into each one.

He stopped suddenly when he came across a hieroglyphic symbol that looked familiar—the symbol on his costume, the symbol of his Kryptonian heritage.

As he was gazing at the monolith, a crippling pain shot through his body. Leaning forward and bracing himself, he peered out the window of his craft to see a faint green glow radiating from the monolith.

Kryptonite!

Trying to get away before the kryptonite could do too much damage, Superman zoomed his ship away from the monolith toward what he thought was the edge of a cliff. When he arrived, however, he was amazed to discover that the cliff actually dropped off into nothingness—he had been exploring only a chunk of what once had been the planet Krypton!

Superman realized that he was trapped in the middle of an asteroid field made up of nothing but kryptonite. Huge chunks of the green rock whizzed by his ship, and as each passed, Superman could feel more and more of the strength draining from his body. Superman was trying desperately to get out of the asteroid field before his strength completely left him when a truck-size chunk of kryptonite slammed into the side of his ship, smashing a section of the hull and throwing Superman to the floor. The damaged portions of the ship grew back, repairing themselves almost immediately.

Superman struggled to get to his feet as the kryptonite asteroids continued their assault. A kryptonite asteroid the size of a golf ball smashed into a window, shattering it.

As the crystals of the window worked to re-form themselves, Superman punched a series of commands into the ship's console and then managed to whisper one word—
"Home."

Taking one last look at the remnants of the home he never knew, Superman crawled back into his sleeping pod as an image of Earth appeared on the ship's console.

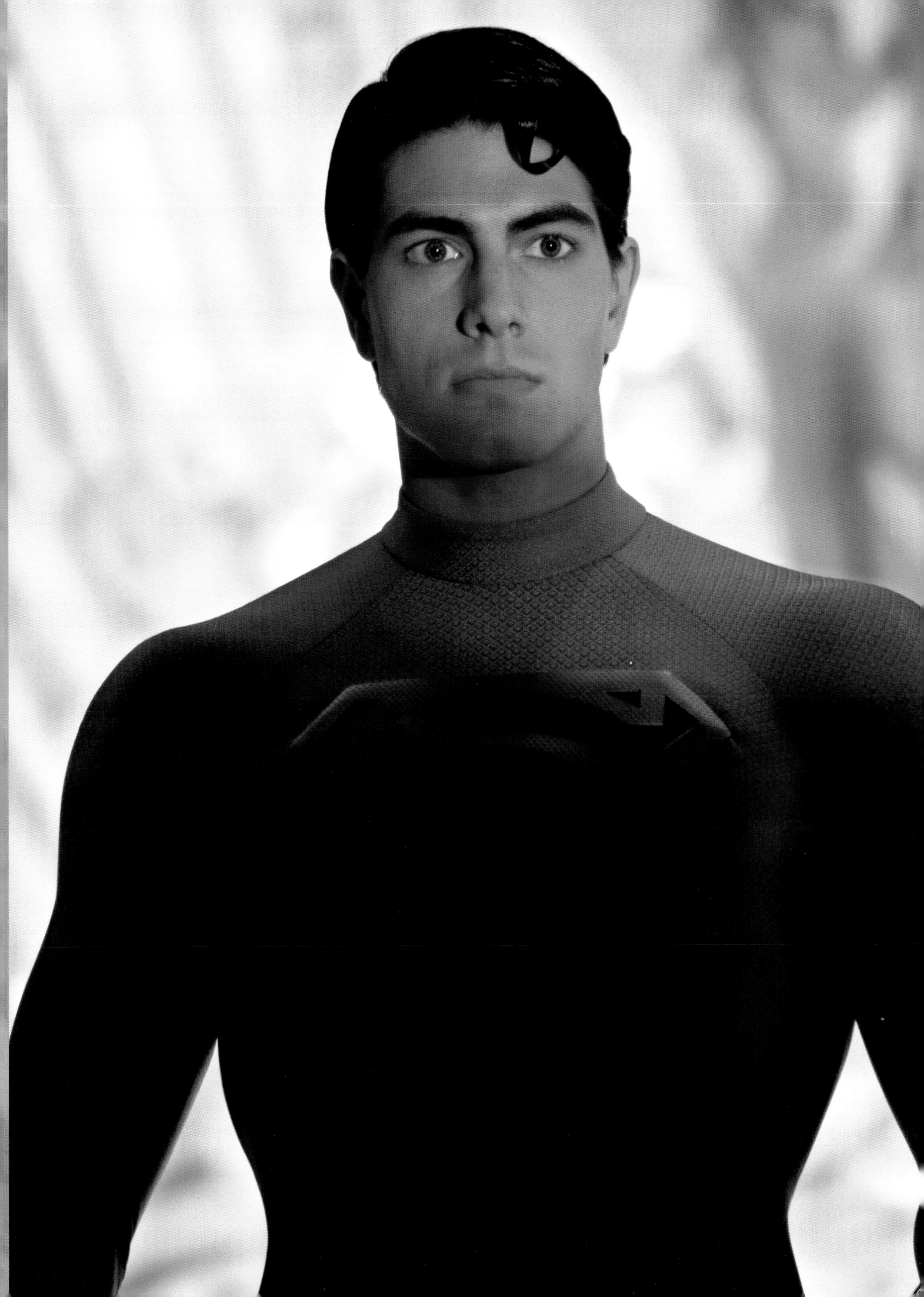

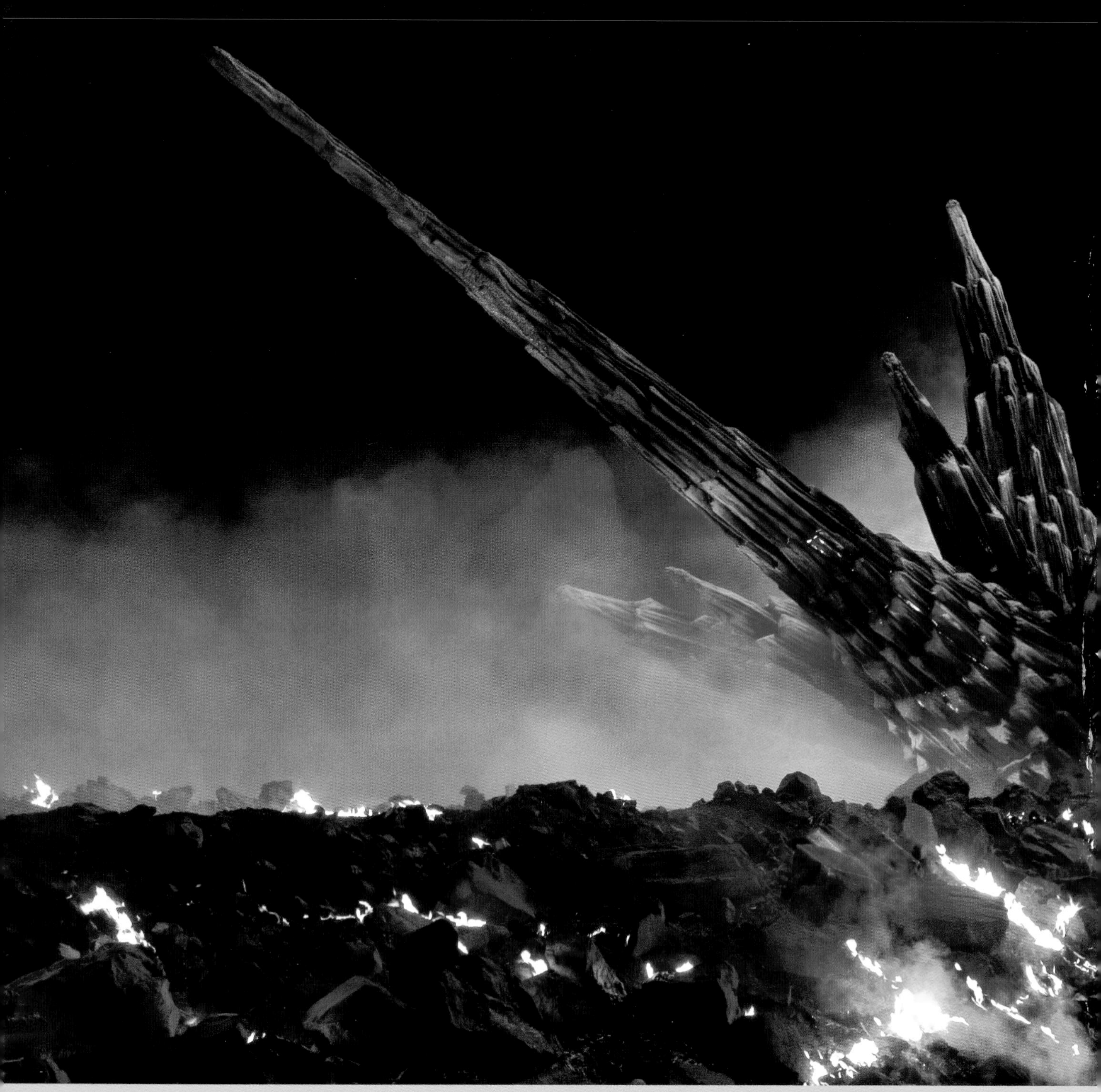
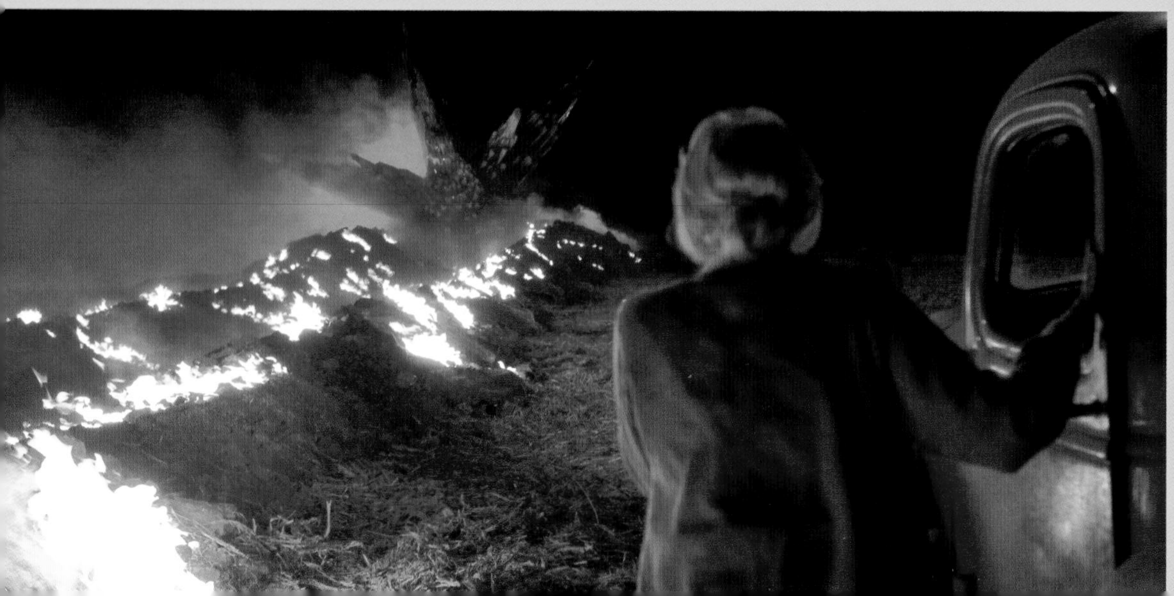
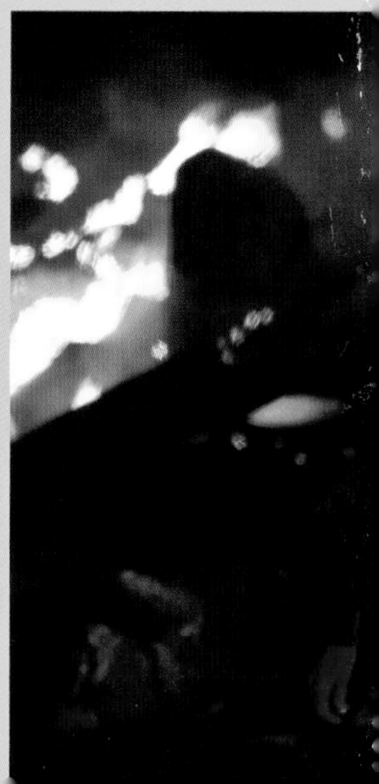

Martha Kent heard a low, deep rumbling. She looked out her kitchen window to see bright red clouds of dust rising as a meteorite slammed into the Earth.

Martha rushed to her pickup truck and followed the trench the meteorite had made until she came to its resting place. There she saw the charred remains of Superman's crystalline ship, still glowing from re-entry.

She jumped as someone touched her from behind.

"Mom . . ." Superman gasped as he collapsed into her arms.

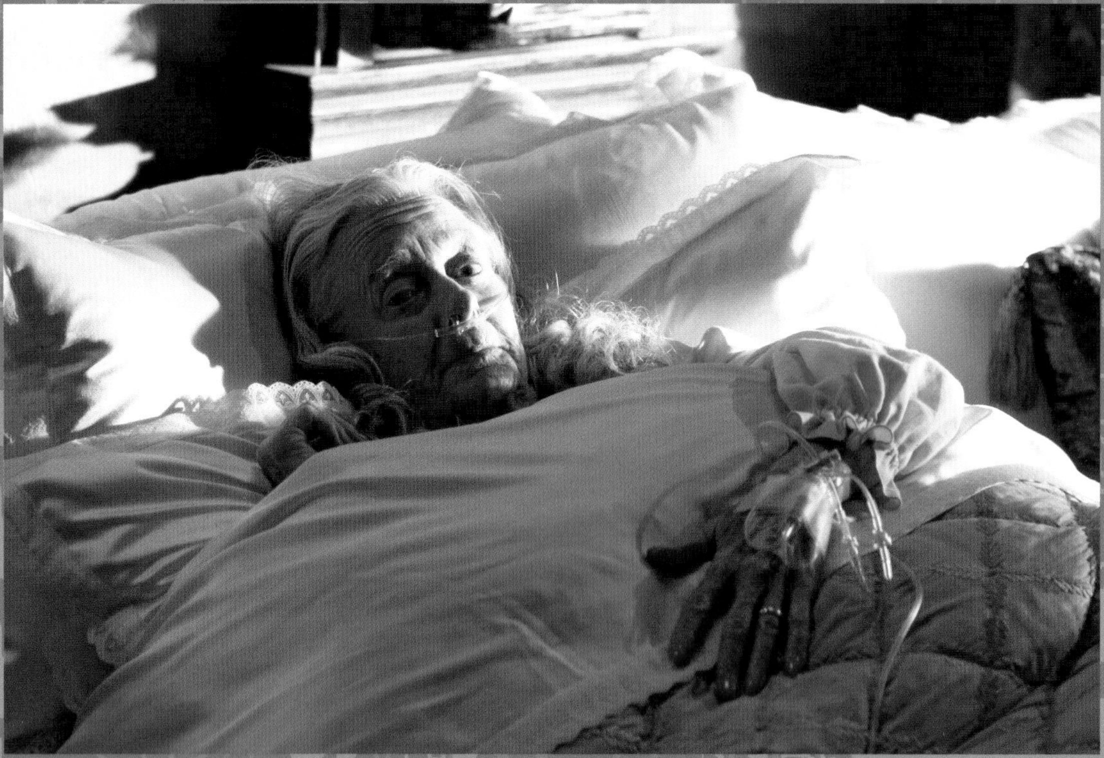

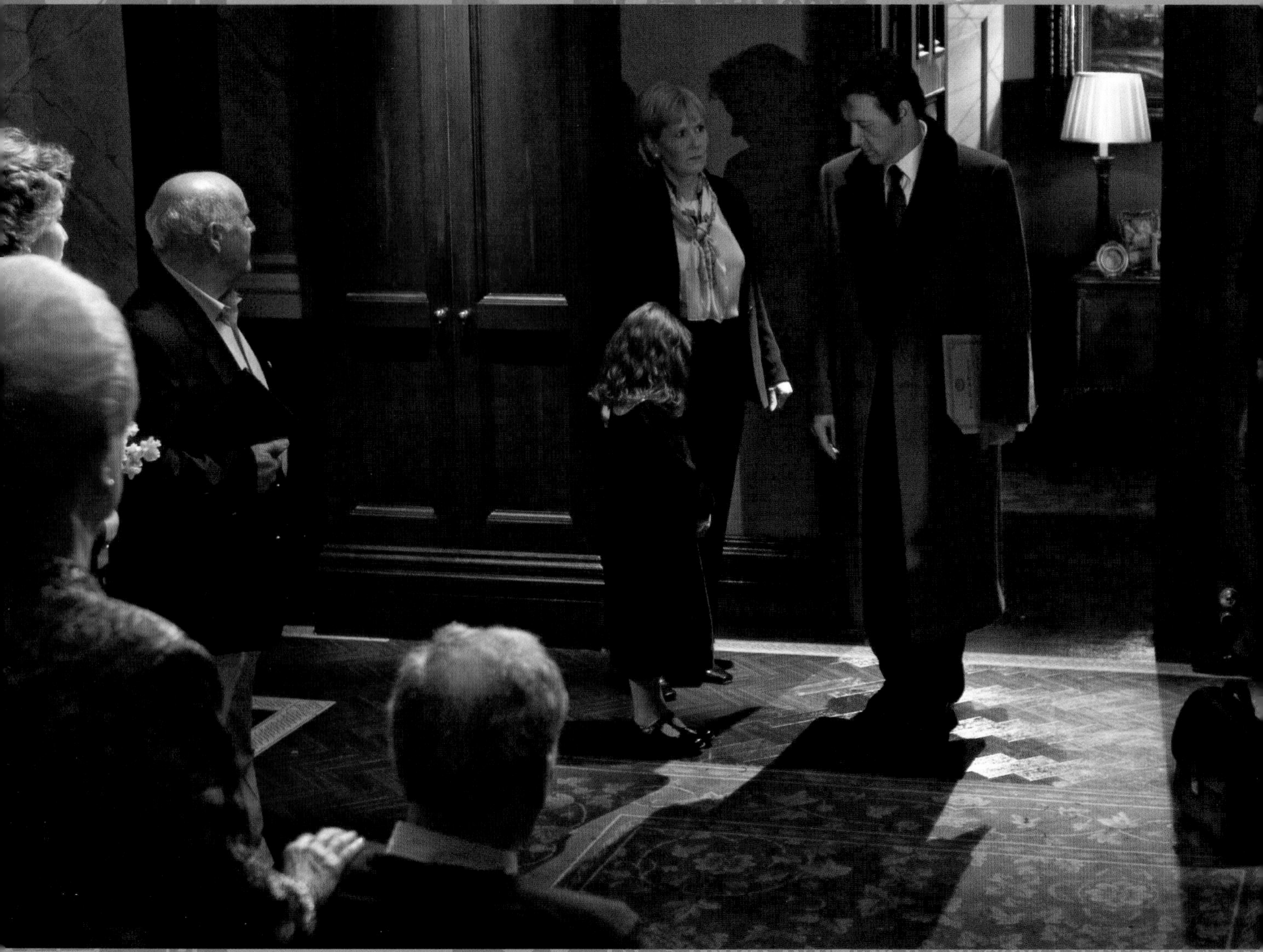

URN OF A HERO!

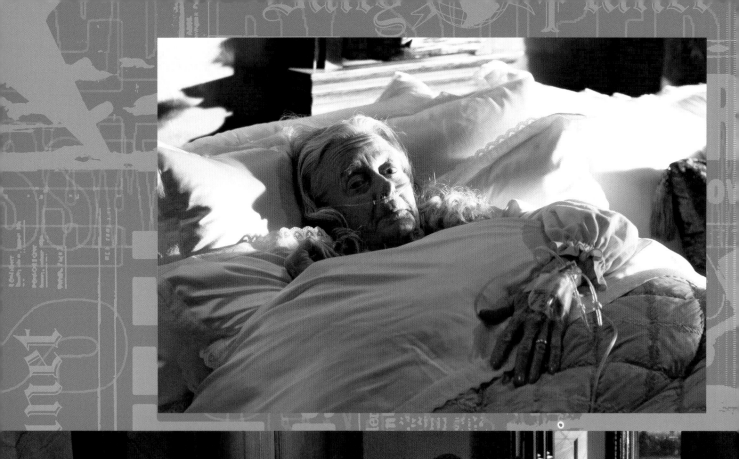

"**In** spite of your past, I know you're a good man," Gertrude Vanderworth said to the man sitting at her bedside in the luxurious Vanderworth mansion. The frail old woman was holding his hand. "And all good men deserve a second chance."

As she spoke, surrounded by the medical equipment that kept her alive, her family was outside, banging on the door to get in. The man pushed her last will and testament into her hands so she could sign it.

"You said that if I helped you get out of prison that you'd take care of me. And you have. You've done so much for me. And that's why you deserve everything."

As she signed her will, she said, "I love you, Lex Luthor." With that, she was gone.

Lex Luthor, criminal mastermind and Superman's sworn archenemy, exited Gertrude's room and stunned her relatives by handing over the will stating that the entire Vanderworth shipping fortune was now his to do with as he pleased.

"You can have this," he joked, ripping the wig from his shiny, bald head and tossing it to a little girl. "The rest is mine."

He then motioned to the maid, who was busy dusting, to join him. He and the maid, who actually was Lex's girlfriend, Kitty Kowalski, then left the shocked family and exited the mansion.

Back on the Kent family farm, Clark Kent was just waking up. He was in his old bedroom, the one he had slept in since his parents had first found him in that meteorite crater so many years ago—before he had discovered that he actually was Superman, a being sent from another planet to protect Earth.

Clark looked up at the ceiling and saw the small stars that had been glued there since he was a child. It was so good to be home!

"Hey, boy," Clark said to the family dog as he rolled over in his bed. Clark was still in pain from his journey, but he

managed to get dressed and head downstairs.

Descending the staircase, Clark looked at the photos from his childhood. They brought back memories—birthday parties, working on the farm with his father, his high school graduation—nothing to suggest that he was actually Superman, a being from another world.

Clark walked outside to take a look at the farm where he had spent so many years. It had fallen into disrepair since his father died. The machinery sat rusted and unused, and the fields of corn were overgrown and untended. Clark took a deep breath of the morning air and then knelt down to run his fingers through the soil. As he did, a flood of childhood memories came rushing back.

When Clark was 15, he had been doing his chores when he fell through the barn roof. The wood roof splintered beneath Clark's feet as he crashed through, he didn't hit the ground— he hovered just above it! He could fly!

Terrified by what he had just experienced, Clark ran out of the barn and into the cornfield. He realized he was running faster than anything he had ever seen before. Everything around him was a blur.

Suddenly he yelled and leapt up into the air! He sailed over the cornstalks and landed, still running. He tried again—and he jumped even higher! Every time he landed, he ran and jumped again, and every time he went higher. He ran with all his might, closed his eyes, and bounded into the air again. He soared even higher than before.

After he landed, Clark opened his eyes and realized he was on top of the old grain silo. He was half a mile away from the farm and had traveled all that way in a matter of seconds!

"Wow!" Clark whispered. He was stunned. How on Earth had he done what he did?

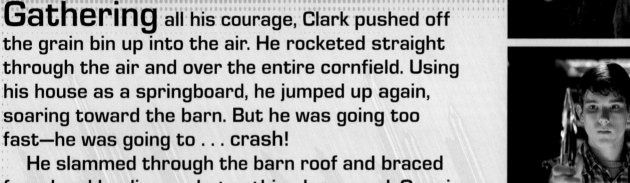

Gathering

Gathering all his courage, Clark pushed off the grain bin up into the air. He rocketed straight through the air and over the entire cornfield. Using his house as a springboard, he jumped up again, soaring toward the barn. But he was going too fast—he was going to . . . crash!

He slammed through the barn roof and braced for a hard landing . . . but nothing happened. Opening his eyes, Clark realized he was hovering above the ground again. He was baffled, so he stood up and fell over on purpose this time. Still he hovered! Then he noticed something else amazing—his glasses had fallen off, yet he could see perfectly. What on Earth was going on?

Clark looked over and noticed a strange handle sticking out from the barn floor. Lowering himself to the ground, he pulled the handle, opening a door in the floor. Peering through the door, Clark saw a set of stairs leading down to an underground room he had never seen before!

He walked down the steps cautiously, not knowing what to expect. There was a large object covered with a tarp. Brimming with curiosity, Clark pulled the tarp away to reveal a crystal structure that looked like a meteor. It was hollow, as if something had been inside. He approached it to get a closer look.

When he peered inside, he discovered a gleaming crystal. It was humming, as if it were calling to him. Clark reached in and picked it up. When he touched it, a white glow flooded the room. He examined it carefully—it was beautiful, like nothing he had ever seen. At that moment Clark knew the crystal was meant for him and that somehow this discovery would explain the amazing things he had experienced that morning. He knew he had to talk to his parents and learn the truth.

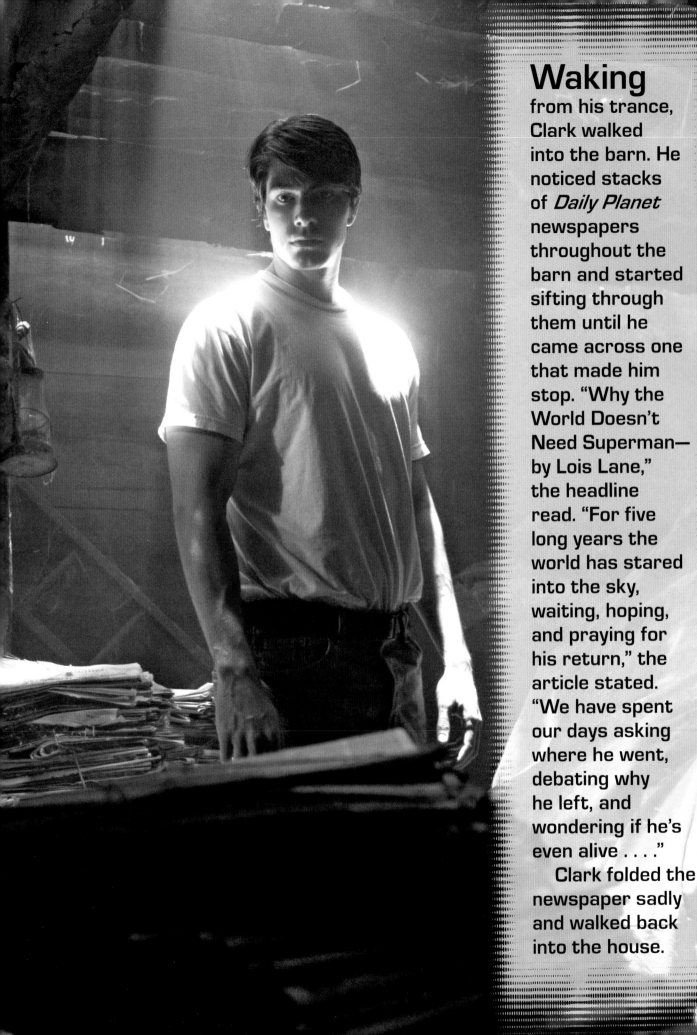

Waking from his trance, Clark walked into the barn. He noticed stacks of *Daily Planet* newspapers throughout the barn and started sifting through them until he came across one that made him stop. "Why the World Doesn't Need Superman— by Lois Lane," the headline read. "For five long years the world has stared into the sky, waiting, hoping, and praying for his return," the article stated. "We have spent our days asking where he went, debating why he left, and wondering if he's even alive . . . ."

Clark folded the newspaper sadly and walked back into the house.

Clark was considering staying at the farm for a while and fixing it up. Lois Lane's article made him feel as if he were no longer needed, and he was tired of leading a secret life, hiding who he really was from his friends.

He had told them all he was going off to explore the world. His mother had sent Lois postcards to make her think that Clark was traveling the globe instead of searching for his home planet. Martha Kent knew that Clark couldn't turn away from his destiny—that wasn't why he was sent to Earth.

"Your father used to say that you were put here for a reason. And we all know it wasn't to work on a farm," Martha said to Clark.

He knew she was right.

Near the North Pole, a yacht named *The Gertrude* was making its way through a nasty storm. Inside, Lex Luthor was surrounded by articles about Superman and the planet Krypton, and was busy reading books on crystals and minerals.

Trying to explain to Kitty what they were doing at the North Pole, Lex said, "Whoever controls technology controls the world."

"We've found something!" one of his men interrupted. He showed Lex the information he had discovered.

"That's it! Drop anchor!" Lex shouted.

Lex and his crew trekked through the icy landscape, Kitty complaining the entire time. One of his men grabbed onto some ice for support, but the ice was warm!

"You were right—there's some sort of unnatural weather pattern keeping it hidden," Stanford, one of Lex Luthor's henchmen, said, looking at his equipment.

"I'm always right," Lex responded.

They had found what they were looking for. They were in front of a huge structure made entirely of the same crystal structures found on Krypton. They had discovered Superman's Fortress of Solitude!

As they explored the Fortress, Kitty noticed a huge chunk of crystal missing from the structure.

"What's that, his garage?" she asked, jokingly.

"You're not that far off, Kitty." Lex lectured. "I heard he took off in a failed attempt to find his home world. If so, he would have had to rely on a craft of some kind, and I'll bet Gertrude's last dollar that's exactly what used to be there."

Lex came across something that looked like a control panel and found that his body heat triggered it. A white crystal pulsed with light. Lex removed the crystal from its container, placing it into a large opening on the panel. The crystal triggered lights throughout the Fortress of Solitude. Whispers echoed all around the structure. Finally, an image of Superman's father, Jor-El, appeared in front of Lex Luthor and his cohorts.

"My son. Over the years, I have instructed you in all the languages, arts, and sciences of Earth, as well as those of your home world, Krypton. There are, no doubt, more questions to be asked. So, my son, speak."

Lex, pretending to be Superman, said: "Tell me everything, starting with the crystals."

Clark Kent had been lucky—his former boss, Perry White, was in need of a reporter at the *Daily Planet*, so Clark got his job back.

Jimmy Olsen, a staff photographer for the *Daily Planet*, was excited to see Clark, and filled him in on all that had been going on since Clark left to "explore the world."

A press conference was being shown on the TV in the newsroom—something big was happening. Lois was there, asking a NASA spokesperson some tough questions. The TV then cut to an image of a Boeing 777 with a space shuttle on its back. Lois Lane was aboard the jet!

"Jimmy, what is this all about?" Clark asked.

"It's the first dual-craft launch of an orbital shuttle using onboard SRBs instead of external fuel tanks. They're going to launch it off the back of a jet!" Jimmy explained.

"Sounds dangerous," said Clark.

Clark now was eyeing Lois's desk. He saw a card that read: "Lois Lane, as a recipient of this year's Pulitzer Prize, you are formally invited to the award ceremony." He also noticed photographs of Lois with a man and small boy, and a child's artwork that said, "To Mom." Upset, Clark asked Jimmy about it. Jimmy explained that Lois had a child but was not married.

Clark was trying to forget about what he had seen, so he and Jimmy went to a diner across the street from the Daily Planet to eat lunch and catch up.

"**This** place is so tacky. Lex, why are we back here?" Kitty asked in disgust as she and Lex walked through the Vanderworth mansion.

"Kitty, while you were doing your nails, I was unlocking the secrets of one of the most advanced civilizations in the universe," Lex Luthor responded. "You see, unlike our clunky earth-bound methods of construction, the technology of Krypton was based on manipulating the growth of crystals." As the two headed down into the basement, Lex continued: "Cities, vehicles, weapons. Entire continents! All grown, not built. To think, one could create a new world with such a simple little object." With that, he removed the white crystal he had discovered in the Fortress of Solitude. "It's like a seed. All we need is water."

"Like sea monkeys!" Kitty exclaimed.

"Yes," Lex agreed. "Like sea monkeys."

With a flip of a light switch, Lex revealed a sprawling and incredibly detailed model train set, complete with miniature people and cities. Above the set planes and jets circled, suspended by wires.

Peering through a microscope, Stanford used a tiny saw to carve a sliver from the Kryptonian crystal. As he carried it to Lex, he tripped over a wire and sent the sliver flying right into a lake on the model. With a hiss, all the power in the mansion went out.

The power outage spread across Metropolis, leaving the entire city in darkness. As the power outage spread, it reached the jet carrying the space shuttle. As the lights in the jet flickered off, the passengers panicked, but the NASA spokesperson remained calm.

At NASA's mission control, the flight commander told the crew aboard the passenger plane that the shuttle launch would have to be cancelled because of the power outage. But when the crew tried to turn off the shuttle engines and abort the launch, they realized that their controls weren't responding and there was nothing they could do to separate the jet from the space shuttle! The launch would continue whether they wanted it to or not!

As the passenger plane and space shuttle climbed higher and higher, they experienced a sonic boom—the deafening explosion rattled the cabin. Primary boosters on the shuttle ignited and began to melt the jet's tail. Inside the plane, the NASA spokesperson and reporters screamed as oxygen masks dropped from the ceiling.

Back at the diner, Clark saw what was happening on one of the diner's TVs and sprang into action. He leapt from his seat and raced to change into Superman. As he ran into an alley and pulled his shirt open, he realized he had left his costume in a suitcase back at the Daily Planet! He raced back into the office and changed into his Superman uniform, slipping past reporters and editors who were too busy watching what was happening on TV to notice him flying out a window.

The shuttle and jet approached the mesosphere as Superman sped toward the out-of-control crafts. Just as he approached them, the shuttle's booster rockets fired, blowing the jet's tail completely off and sending Superman spiraling backward!

Superman struggled to regain control so he could catch up to the jet and pry it loose from the shuttle. Breaking the sound barrier, Superman soared back toward the jet and shuttle.

Inside the jet, Lois strapped herself in. Looking out the window, she saw the blue sky fading to black and then Superman speeding past. Unsure of herself, she did a double take—did she really see that?

Outside, Superman landed on the roof of the jet, placing himself between it and the shuttle. Superman used all his strength to pry the two apart. Couplings holding the crafts together snapped under his power, and the vehicles separated. With all his might, Superman pushed the shuttle up and away from the jet, allowing it to soar safely into space.

"We have lift-off. I mean, we're in orbit. Everything's okay!" the shuttle commander reported to mission control.

The passengers aboard the jet felt a momentary sense of calm once they detached from the shuttle, and then realized their worries were far from over as the plane started to plummet back toward Earth!

Spiraling out of control, the jet sped toward the ground as Superman raced to catch it. He tried to grab onto the right wing to slow the descending craft, but it was no use—the wing just snapped off. Pieces of the jet flew everywhere as it raced closer and closer to the ground.

Finally, Superman braced himself against the nose of the jet, pushing with all his might in an attempt to slow the plane's fall.

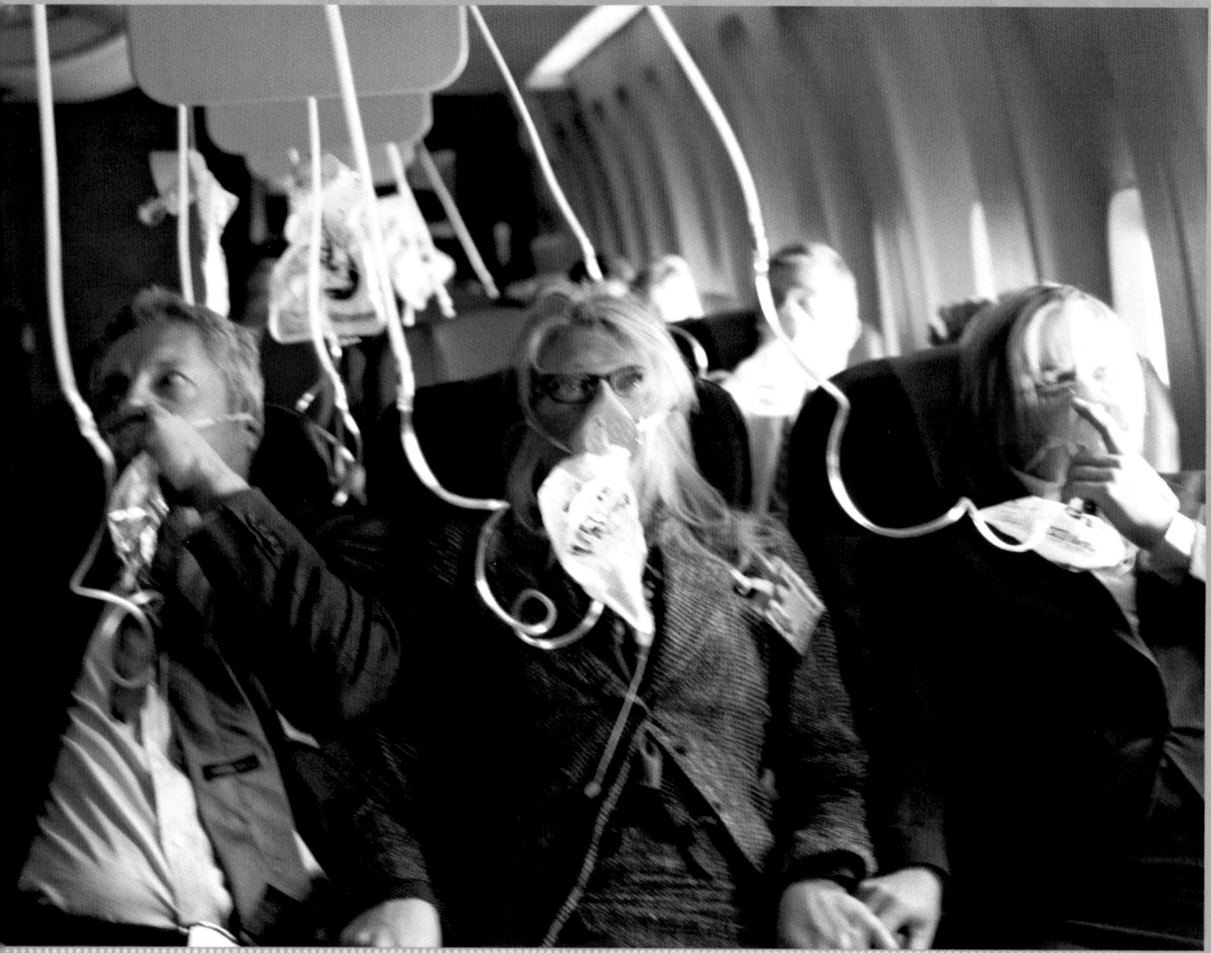

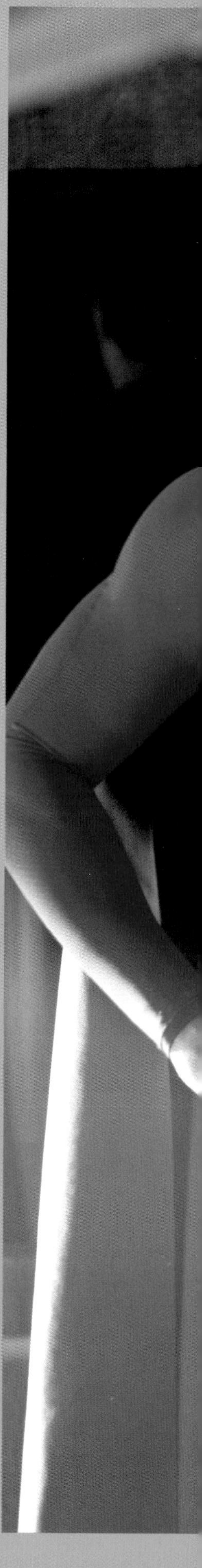

As the batter hit a fly ball, the spectators at a baseball stadium watched it soar upward when their eyes caught sight of Superman pushing against the nose of the spiraling jet. All the players on the field rushed out of the way as Superman and the jet sped toward the baseball diamond.

Inside the jet, Lois closed her eyes. Everyone around her screamed hysterically. They were doomed.

Superman looked behind him and saw the baseball diamond. With one last shove, he pushed with all his strength, and the jet's descent ended. Metallic groans filled the air as Superman stopped the falling plane a few feet above the ground. Gently, Superman lowered the damaged jet onto the grass.

Inside, the stunned passengers didn't know what to think. What had happened? As the rescue slide inflated, Superman stepped inside. "Is everyone all right?" he asked. "I suggest you all stay in your seats until medical attention arrives."

Out from behind a seat came a shocked Lois Lane. She hadn't seen Superman in years, and here he was right in front of her!

"Are you okay?" Superman asked as she stood up nervously. Lois opened her mouth to say something, but couldn't get anything out.

Superman made sure she was okay, and then said, "I hope this incident hasn't put any of you off flying. Statistically speaking, it's still the safest way to travel."

And with that, he stepped off the jet.

The crowd at the baseball stadium sat in stunned silence while Superman's image flashing on the huge monitors above the seats. As the spectators began to realize what they had just witnessed, their silence transformed into thunderous applause—Superman was back!

Meanwhile, back at the Vanderworth mansion, there was chaos. The model train set was a smoky ruin. Where miniature cities had been, huge crystalline structures had sprouted that were identical to those in the Fortress of Solitude. The crystal shards shot straight up through the ceiling and spread roots down through the floor.

"Lex, your little crystal broke everything," Kitty said.

"Yes, so it did." Lex whispered.

Superman was big news the next day, and Perry White wanted all the angles covered. He assigned Lois the task of getting an exclusive interview with Superman, but she protested. She had more important things to investigate—specifically, the unexplained blackout that had caused so much trouble throughout the city.

"The story isn't about the blackout! It's about Superman!" Perry lectured.

As Lois left Perry's office, she told him she would get the Superman story, but she really was off to work on another story—the blackout.

Then she saw Clark.

"Clark! Welcome back!" she said.

Clark tried to make small talk but was nervous—he hadn't seen her in a long time. Not only did Lois have a son, she also had a boyfriend—Richard White, nephew of Perry White, and a reporter for the *Daily Planet*.

Lex Luthor was furious about Superman's return. How had he managed to return to Earth?

Pacing aboard his yacht, which was docked near the Vanderworth mansion, Lex was joined by his henchmen. They had just returned from stealing a rocket and its launcher and were carrying it in a large crate.

"So, what are we going to do?" Stanford asked.

"You're going to modify it according to the plans and attach it to the stern of the ship."

"No, I mean about him!" Stanford said, referring to Superman. He and Lex had worked long and hard to make it seem as if there were life on Krypton, and he was angry that Superman had managed to return to Earth in one piece.

Then Lex saw it—a newpaper headline that gave him the answer. "WORLD'S LARGEST COLLECTION OF METEORITES ON DISPLAY AT METROPOLIS MUSEUM OF NATURAL HISTORY."

"**Hey**, Clark. How's your first week back at work?" Lois asked at the Daily Planet the next morning.

"It's okay. Kind of like riding a bike," Clark responded.

As the two kept talking, the conversation came to Superman. Lois had been hurt that Superman had left without saying goodbye to her.

"Well, maybe saying goodbye was so hard because he didn't know if it would be goodbye for a little while, or goodbye forever," Clark said sympathetically.

"What's so difficult about it?" Lois said, upset.

Trying to change the subject, Clark asked if she would like to have lunch. Lois couldn't, but she invited him out to her home in the suburbs for dinner instead.

Superman was flying through the city when he happened upon Lois' home. He heard her inside talking to Richard about Superman's return. He heard Lois tell Richard that she was no longer in love with Superman. Saddened, Superman flew high into the sky.

As Superman flew higher, he heard an alarm go off—he swooped back down and caught four robbers on the roof of a bank. They were throwing bags of money into a helicopter and were getting ready to take off. The bank was surrounded by police officers on the ground. There was no way the robbers were going to give up—they pulled a large machine gun out of a crate and were getting ready to open fire on the police when two bank security guards sneaked up behind them and started shooting. As the robbers turned to fire back, Superman landed between them and deflected the bullets!

"What took you so long?" the bank security guards asked when the SWAT team finally burst onto the roof.

The SWAT team couldn't believe what they saw—each of the robbers had been tied up with a bent helicopter blade and were swaying in the breeze.

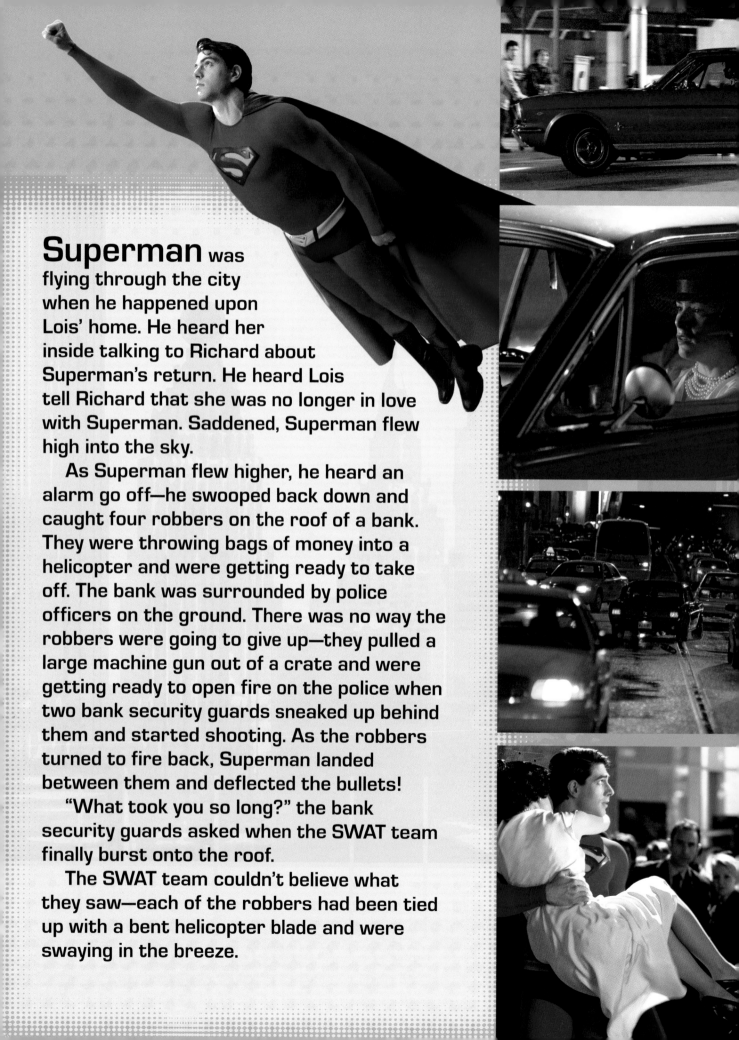

Across town, a car completely out of control crashed through the streets. The woman behind the steering wheel screamed hysterically, spinning the wheel to avoid hitting people. As the car careened through the panicked streets, it bounded into a park, racing around benches and trees as people scattered to get out of the way.

Surely the car was going to crash, but suddenly the driver realized she was hovering above the park! As her car descended gently to the ground, she saw that Superman had come to her rescue.

"Miss, are you all right?" Superman asked the driver.

"My heart!" the driver screamed. As she collapsed, Superman caught her in his arms.

It was Kitty Kowalski.

"Heart palpitation! I have a heart palpitation and a murmur!"

Superman tried to tell her that he couldn't see anything wrong with her, but she begged him to take her to the hospital.

At the same time, Lex and his men were getting off a tour bus. They were dressed as tourists, complete with souvenir T-shirts and disposable cameras. They were in front of the Metropolis Museum of Natural History.

"I'm sorry, we close in **10** minutes," the security guard warned.

"That's plenty of time—we're only interested in one exhibit," Lex said as he and his men rushed into the museum.

At the meteorite exhibit, they all took pictures with their cameras until they came across a meteorite from Addis Ababa. This was the one!

Lex broke the case and grabbed the meteorite, and alarms sounded throughout the museum. As the guards rushed in, Lex's henchmen turned to take their pictures—zap! The cameras were actually stun guns, and the guards slumped to the floor.

Triumphantly, Lex chipped at the meteorite's exterior. As the faint green glow became more prominent, Lex knew he had what he wanted—kryptonite!

Back on his yacht, Lex stood in front of a map of the world, placing a pin at the intersection of several lines, when Kitty walked in.

"I was going to pretend the brakes were out, like we talked about. PRETEND! You didn't have to cut them!" Kitty screamed. "What are those lines?" she asked, changing the subject, as usual.

"Those lines? They are 12 fault lines. As for the pin," he said. "The pin is where we're going."

Up on the bridge, Stanford had the rocket on the counter, with all of its inner parts removed. He looked at the hollow compartment on the rocket and then measured the meteor they had stolen. Most of its outer shell had been chipped away, revealing a strong inner layer of kryptonite.

As Stanford continued to cut into the meteor, Lex noticed a shard of kryptonite that had fallen onto the counter. He picked it up and slipped it into his pocket.

At the Daily Planet, Perry White had made some changes. Clark and Lois now were working together on the blackout story, and Richard was going to help Lois on the Superman story.

Lois and Clark were beginning to work when Lois said she needed a break. She left Clark to go up to the roof for some fresh air. While she was on her way, Clark changed into his Superman uniform and surprised Lois as she stepped out the door.

As the two began to talk, Lois asked him about where he had gone and what he had hoped to find. Soon the conversation turned more personal—Superman brought up the article that had won Lois the Pulitzer Prize.

"Why did you write it?" Superman asked.

After Lois explained, he apologized for hurting her.

"You didn't hurt me. You didn't hurt any of us. You just helped us find the strength to take care of ourselves. That's why I wrote the article— the world doesn't need a savior."

Superman

took Lois into his arms and they flew high into the sky. He wanted to show her something. They had flown so high that everything was silent. "What do you hear?" Superman asked seriously.

"Nothing. It's quiet." Lois replied.

"Do you know what I hear? Everything. You said the world doesn't need a savior—but every day I hear people crying out for one. I'm sorry I left you, Lois. I'll take you back now."

He took Lois back to the roof of the Daily Planet building. When she went back into the offices, Superman left for the Fortress of Solitude.

"Father, it's been a long time since I've come to you, but I've never felt so alone," Superman said. He was met with silence. "Father?" He called as he realized something was wrong. The crystal was missing!

During her research on the blackout, Lois had discovered that the power outage originated at the Vanderworth mansion. Lois and her son, Jason, were on their way to the award ceremony where she was to receive her Pulitzer Prize when she decided to take a small detour to investigate.

She and Jason approached the mansion, but no one answered her knock. Then she heard music coming from the yacht docked behind the mansion. As she and Jason searched for someone aboard the ship, she noticed the box of wigs—Lex Luthor's wigs, she realized with horror.

"This was a bad idea. We have to get out of here," she whispered. Then the yacht's motor roared to life, and the craft pulled away from the dock. Lois grabbed Jason and ran for the door. When she opened it, she was face to face with Lex.

As the yacht churned out to sea, Lex filled Lois in on his dastardly plot, revealing everything to her.

He was planning to grow the crystal he had taken from the Fortress of Solitude into a huge continent that would be virtually indestructible! With the crystal at his disposal, he could create weapons and vehicles beyond any technology the Earth had ever seen.

"For lack of a better name, the new continent is called New Krypton. An extinct world, reborn on our own," he said smugly.

As he continued, Lex showed Lois the point on the map that indicated where they were headed. The point was off the coast of Metropolis.

"But that's directly above a fault line!" Lois shrieked. "If you built something there, you could cause an earthquake. Thousands of people would die!"

"Millions. Once again, the press underestimates me," Lex responded.

"Superman will never allow you to get away with this," Lois snapped.

"Wrong!" said Lex as he revealed a glowing green shard of kryptonite.

As Lex spoke, he revealed that he knew about Superman's trip to Krypton.

"How would you know he went back to find Krypton? He only told me, and that hasn't been published yet!" Lois said. Then it dawned on her. The photos, the theories about Krypton surviving—they all had been Lex Luthor's plot to get rid of Superman!

The ship arrived at the coordinates on Lex's map. Lex took the kryptonite and a shard of the white crystal from Superman's fortress and placed them together in the stolen rocket.

"This is going to be good," he said, leaving Lois and Jason in the room with his thug Brutus.

Up on deck Lex finished securing the crystals in the rocket's compartment and inserted the rocket into the launcher.

"Ready, boss?" Stanford asked. With a nod from Lex, the rocket was off.

Zoom! The rocket sailed through the sky and arced downward, slamming into the water. As it disappeared into the depths, an eerie glow followed it down. As the rocket hit the ocean floor, it caused another blackout, rippling from the ship through Metropolis.

Inside the rocket the crystal started to grow, branching out, melding with the kryptonite. The crystal structure grew so large that it shattered the rocket. The crystal structure continued to grow, digging deep into a chasm in the ocean floor while punching upward to burst through the water's surface and explode into the sky.

Lois, meanwhile, had managed to send a fax that detailed the yacht's coordinates to the Daily Planet bullpen before Brutus unplugged the fax machine. After a struggle, Lois and Jason were locked in the pantry aboard the yacht so they wouldn't cause any more trouble.

At the Daily Planet, Jimmy, Richard, and Clark stared at the fax and realized that it contained sea coordinates, and sprang into action.

Richard told Jimmy to call the Coast Guard and to tell Perry that he would take his seaplane. He asked Clark to join him.

"No thanks, I get airsick," Clark said, before running to the elevator bank. Whoosh! Through the elevator shaft, Superman tore out of the Daily Planet building and to the coordinates Lois had faxed.

As he soared out of the city and over the water, he realized something much worse was happening—using his X-ray vision, he peered into the water and saw the ocean floor splitting open. The crack was traveling fast, right toward Metropolis! If he didn't stop it, the entire city would be destroyed!

Perry was asking Jimmy about the fax when they heard the rumbling. It seemed faint at first, but then hundreds of car alarms went off and the building began to tremble.

Outside, debris rained down all over the city as the split in the Earth neared land. Huge cracks ripped through the city streets. Manhole covers and cars exploded everywhere.

As Superman zoomed into the city, two skyscrapers began to crumble from the strain. Thinking fast, he lifted a huge crane and propped it between the two buildings, keeping them from crashing down onto the hysterical crowd below.

Perry White and his staff stood outside the Daily Planet building while chaos reigned all around them. The giant Daily Planet globe that sat atop the building came loose and began to fall. Just as it was about to slam into the street, Superman caught it and placed it gently on the ground.

"Superman—Perry White. *Daily Planet*. What's happening?" Perry asked, trying to get an exclusive.

Superman told him to warn everyone to get as far away from the buildings as possible.

"How can we avoid buildings? This is a city!" Perry exclaimed.

"If I don't do something fast, there won't be a city left," Superman said as he took off.

Lex and his crew were clambering aboard their helicopter when a tidal wave slammed into the yacht, engulfing it in water.

As the yacht listed in the ocean, water spilled through cracks into the pantry, where Lois and Jason were locked in. The water rose higher and higher, until it reached Lois' neck.

"Help!" Lois screamed. Just then the door ripped open. Richard had found them with his seaplane!

As they hugged, a huge crystal column shot out of the ocean and pierced the ship's hull, turning the craft upside down as the crystal grew larger. As the ship was raised out of the water, it split in half, sending the broken ship tumbling back into the ocean. The pantry door flew open again for a moment. As Lois raced to catch it, she was knocked unconscious. Water spewed into the tiny room, filling it almost to the ceiling. Just as they were about to give up hope, Superman burst in and carried them to safety.

They stared in awe—all around them were enormous crystal columns that seemed to have grown out of nowhere!

"Take them out of here—and don't come back," Superman said to Richard as they climbed safely into the seaplane.

Superman flew to the heart of the crystal formation when suddenly it dawned on him—it looked just like Krypton! He swooped down toward the center of the structures and saw the familiar circle of monoliths, exactly like the ones he had seen in space. In the center of the monoliths was a structure that looked almost identical to the Fortress of Solitude. Resting next to it was Lex's helicopter.

However, unlike Krypton, Superman felt life all around him here.

"See anything familiar?" Lex Luthor asked, sneering.

"I don't have time for this. You have something that belongs to me, Luthor," Superman said, storming toward Lex to get his crystal back.

BAM! Lex punched Superman in the face, knocking him to the ground. In shock, Superman realized that his nose was bleeding!

Onboard the seaplane Lois had regained consciousness.

"It's all right. We're safe," Richard said.

Remembering the kryptonite, Lois screamed. "Richard, we have to turn around!" Nodding in agreement, Richard flew back toward the crystals.

Meanwhile, Lex continued his assault on Superman.

"I didn't send you to die on Krypton just to have you come back and stop me now!"

All at once Superman realized that he had been tricked! "You . . . why?"

"You robbed me of five years of my life," Lex spat. "I just returned the favor."

As Superman thought about the years of his life he had wasted in hopes of finding Krypton, he realized he was getting sicker and sicker.

"Didn't your mother ever tell you to look before you leap?" Lex taunted.

Superman used his fading X-ray vision and discovered that the entire crystal structure was filled with kryptonite. It was draining all the energy from his body!

"Kryptonite. Amazing, isn't it?" Lex laughed as Superman writhed in pain.

"**Fly!** Come on, fly!" Luthor shouted as he kicked Superman.

Lex's henchmen surrounded Superman. As they pummeled him, Superman drained the last of his strength using his X-ray vision to locate his father's crystal. It was deep inside a console, surrounded by kryptonite. Soon after, his X-ray vision faded. His power was gone.

"You can't go back home, and soon you won't be able to live here, either. There's no place for you anymore, Superman."

As Lex continued his assault, Superman gathered his last remaining strength and dragged himself toward the ledge of the crystal structure. He finally found himself at the edge of a steep cliff that dropped off straight into the ocean.

Superman screamed in pain as Lex stabbed him in the back with the shard of kryptonite. He looked over the ledge, then threw himself into the water.

"So long, Superman," Lex Luthor said, with an evil laugh.

Superman plunged deep into the water and tumbled downward. He struggled to pull out the shard of kryptonite that was embedded in his back, but he couldn't reach it.

All around him crystals were growing in every direction. The faint glow of green from the growing kryptonite illuminated the water around him. Superman struggled to swim to the surface, but he was too weak to move. A mesh of crystals quickly began to encase him!

Above the water Richard circled in the seaplane around the area where Superman had fallen into the ocean. Lois threw open the door of the seaplane and jumped into the raging waters as soon as the plane touched down!

As Lois reached Superman, one last bubble of air escaped from his mouth. Lois grabbed onto Superman's cape and dragged him away from the crystals. She gasped for air as she surfaced with Superman in her arms.

"Wake up! Come on, wake up!" Lois screamed.

Superman came to and gasped, "Kryptonite. There's kryptonite in the crystals."

Lois and Richard knew they had to get Superman away from the crystals if there was any chance of saving him, but the water was too choppy for the plane to take off.

Around them crystal pillars rose fast. The plane barely made it through two giant formations that shot out of the water.

"Seatbelts!" Richard shouted as he maneuvered through the growing crystal columns.

Just when they thought they were safe, several crystal columns grew beneath them. The plane was now thousands of feet above the ocean—and heading toward a waterfall! They almost tumbled over the waterfall, but the plane managed to catch a strong air current and remained airborne.

Then Lois noticed the shard of kryptonite in Superman's back. She pulled it out and threw it from the plane.

Superman slowly began to regain strength. Out the window he saw New Krypton—still growing. Soon it would take over everything!

"I have to go back," Superman said firmly. "Goodbye, Lois." He flew out of the plane and toward New Krypton. As he flew, the warm yellow light of Earth's sun helped him regain the superstrength the kryptonite had drained from his body. When he was strong enough again, he dove straight into the ocean.

Superman used heat vision to melt the Earth's crust as he disappeared under the ocean floor.

Lex, Kitty, and the crew felt the crystal structure start to rumble all around them. They looked up to see the horizon moving—they were rising into the air!

"NO!" Lex screamed as huge crystal structures began to shatter all around him. "Get to the helicopter. Now!"

They all piled into the helicopter, and Lex, panic-stricken, started

the engines. The helicopter roared to life, but too late—the ground beneath it crumbled away. It plummeted into the forming chasm below. Soon, however, Lex gained control of the helicopter and escaped, looking on in horror as New Krypton lifted higher into the sky.

Huge waves rippled outward as the enormous mass of crystals rose out of the ocean. When its base broke the surface, it was encased in a mass of brown, rocky earth—and below it was Superman!

Higher and higher Superman flew with New Krypton overhead as giant chunks of earth fell off, exposing kryptonite.

In agony Superman drew on the last ounce of his strength as he entered space with the giant crystal formation. With a final burst of power, Superman hurled the structure off into deep space.

Unconscious, Superman descended to Earth. Faster and faster he fell, until the air around him blazed bright orange as he re-entered Earth's atmosphere.

An orange streak shot across the sky high above Metropolis, hurling closer and closer, until WHAM! Superman landed in a park, sending debris flying hundreds of feet into the air.

As the dust cleared, there was a monstrous crater. Superman had landed.

Superman was still unconscious when he was finally removed from the crater his impact had created. He was rushed to the hospital, where he remained unconscious for some time.

Lois Lane visited Superman in the hospital. She realized she had been wrong about the world not needing him—now, more than ever, the world needed Superman.

When he finally recovered, Superman let Lois know that he was all right. He also told her that he would never leave her again. He knew now that Earth was—and always would be—his home.

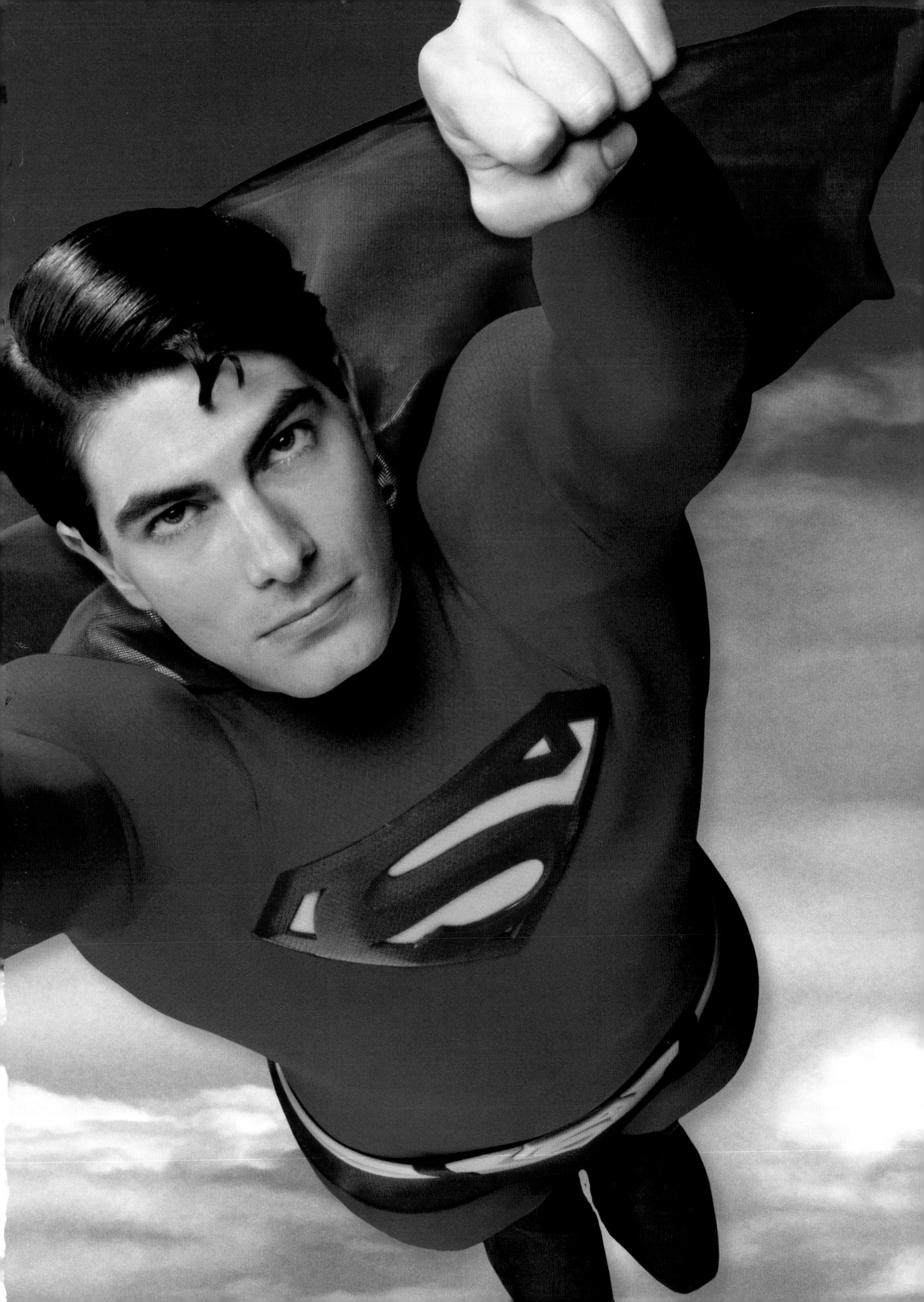

AVAILABLE
WHERE QUALITY
BOOKS ARE SOLD.

I CAN FIND IT!

**COLOR & ACTIVITY
CRAYONS**

**COLOR & ACTIVITY
STICKERS**

**COLOR & ACTIVITY
PAINTS**

**COLOR & ACTIVITY
TATTOOS**

**THE LAST SON
OF KRYPTON**

I AM SUPERMAN!

BE A HERO!

**DELUXE SOUND
STORY BOOK**

**EARTHQUAKE IN
METROPOLIS!**

**COMING
HOME**

SUPERMAN, the DC Logo and all related
names, characters and elements are trademarks
of DC Comics ©2006.
WB Shield: TM & © Warner Bros. Entertainment Inc.
©2006 Meredith Corporation. All rights reserved.

CLD0104_0406